The search for the basketball begins!

The assistant had left the gym. The guard was still standing by the side door. Cam told him they had looked under the bleachers but did not find the basketball.

"Max, Amy, Jane," the guard said into his speaker. "The ball is not under the bleachers. I don't think it's in here."

He held his hand to the earpiece. He listened for a moment.

"Yes, Max," he said. "I'll watch the gym and the door. No one will leave here with that ball."

The guard turned to Cam and Eric. "Why don't you go to the cafeteria. It's a real party with lots of ice cream and cake. Don't worry. We'll find that basketball."

Cam and Eric walked toward the cafeteria.

"He's wrong," Eric whispered to Cam as they walked. "They won't find that basketball. We will!"

CASE #29

The
Basketball Mystery

David A. Adler
Illustrated by Joy Allen

PUFFIN BOOKS
An Imprint of Penguin Group (USA) Inc.

PUFFIN BOOKS
Published by the Penguin Group
Penguin Young Readers Group, 345 Hudson Street, New York, New York 10014, U.S.A.
Penguin Group (Canada), 90 Eglinton Avenue East, Suite 700,
Toronto, Ontario, Canada M4P 2Y3 (a division of Pearson Penguin Canada Inc.)
Penguin Books Ltd, 80 Strand, London WC2R 0RL, England
Penguin Ireland, 25 St Stephen's Green, Dublin 2, Ireland
(a division of Penguin Books Ltd)
Penguin Group (Australia), 250 Camberwell Road, Camberwell, Victoria 3124, Australia
(a division of Pearson Australia Group Pty Ltd)
Penguin Books India Pvt Ltd, 11 Community Centre,
Panchsheel Park, New Delhi - 110 017, India
Penguin Group (NZ), 67 Apollo Drive, Rosedale, North Shore 0632, New Zealand
(a division of Pearson New Zealand Ltd)
Penguin Books (South Africa) (Pty) Ltd, 24 Sturdee Avenue,
Rosebank, Johannesburg 2196, South Africa

Registered Offices: Penguin Books Ltd, 80 Strand, London WC2R 0RL, England

First published in the United States of America by Viking,
a division of Penguin Young Readers Group, 2009
Published by Puffin Books, a division of Penguin Young Readers Group, 2010

7 9 10 8

THE LIBRARY OF CONGRESS HAS CATALOGED THE VIKING EDITION AS FOLLOWS:
Adler, David A.
Cam Jansen and the basketball mystery / by David A. Adler ;
illustrated by Joy Allen.
p. cm.
Summary: When a special autographed basketball is stolen,
Cam Jansen uses her photographic memory to identify the thief.
ISBN: 978-0-670-01198-8 (hardcover)
[1. Basketball—Fiction. 2. Mystery and detective stories.]
I. Allen, Joy, ill. II. Title.
PZ7.A2615Caabd 2009
[E]—dc22 2008046694

Puffin Books ISBN 978-0-14-241671-6

Printed in the United States of America

To my adorable grandson

Jonathan "Yoni" Alex

—D.A.

To Jeff and his bouncing basketball

coming home each day from the park

—J.A.

Chapter One

"Wow!" Mr. Shelton said. "I look so young!"

Cam, her friend Eric Shelton, and Eric's family were on their way to Hamilton High School. They were going there to watch the last basketball game of the season. It was also the last game for Coach Oscar Jenkins. Eric's parents were sitting on the front seat of the SUV. The children were sitting in the back.

Cam looked at Mr. Shelton. The hair around his ears was mostly gray. His face had lots of wrinkles. Cam didn't think he looked young.

Mr. Shelton turned and said, "Look at how young I am in this picture."

He gave Cam his high school yearbook. It was open to a picture of the basketball team.

"There's Dad," Eric said, and pointed.

Mr. Shelton was wearing a basketball uniform, and he did look young.

Eric said, "Look at the player next to Dad, the one at the end of the bench. That's Danny's father. The man standing in the tie and suit is Coach Jenkins."

"This is a great picture," Cam said.

"Look on the next page," Mr. Shelton said. "There are pictures of us playing basketball."

Cam wanted to remember the pictures. She looked at them. Then she blinked her eyes and said, *"Click!"*

Cam has what people call a photographic memory. It's as if she has pictures in her head of everything she's seen. She always says *"Click!"* when she wants to remember something. Cam says *Click!* is the sound her mental camera makes when it takes a picture.

"Here we are," Mrs. Shelton said.

Mrs. Shelton parked the SUV in the school lot. Cam, Eric, and Eric's twin sisters, Donna and Diane, got out. Mr. Shelton took Eric's brother Howie out of the baby seat. Mrs. Shelton took out a large bag filled with baby things. Mr. Shelton carried Howie and they all walked toward the school.

"Hi!" Danny called to Cam and Eric.

Danny Pace and his father were near the end of a long line of people waiting to get into the school.

"Guess what?" Danny's father asked Mr. Shelton.

Mr. Shelton shook his head. He didn't know what to guess.

"No, really," Mr. Pace said. "Guess what I'm wearing."

"I know," Diane Shelton said. "You're wearing a jacket and shoes and pants."

"No. That's not it."

"Yes," Diane said. "You are wearing all that!"

"Yes, but look what else I'm wearing."

Danny's father opened the top few buttons

of his shirt. Beneath it he had on something orange. "I'm wearing the top from my old basketball uniform. It's tight, but I can still get it on."

"It's real tight," Danny whispered.

"I'm wearing it for luck," Danny's father said. "I want Coach Jenkins to win his last game."

People ahead showed their tickets to the student at the door. They entered the gym. Cam and the others moved up.

Danny's father said to Mr. Shelton, "I bet you don't remember the number on my uniform."

Mr. Shelton thought for a moment. Then he shook his head. He didn't remember it.

Cam said, "I bet I know it."

Cam closed her eyes and said, *"Click!"* Then she said, "I'm looking at the pictures in the yearbook. Mr. Pace's number was twenty-four. Mr. Shelton's number was eighteen."

"That's right," Danny's father said. "You really have an amazing memory."

Cam's real name is Jennifer, but because

of her photographic memory people started calling her "The Camera." Soon "The Camera" became just "Cam."

"Open your eyes," Eric told Cam. "It's almost our turn to go in."

Cam opened her eyes. She and the others moved up.

A student was standing by the door. She wore a paper orange Hamilton Helper sash.

"I played for Coach Jenkins," Danny's father told the helper. "Look, I'm wearing my uniform."

He gave her two tickets.

The girl smiled. "I hope you'll stay after the game for the party," she said. "It's for Coach, and it's in the cafeteria."

Mr. Shelton gave her a bunch of tickets. Then Cam and all the Sheltons entered the gym. The game was about to begin.

Chapter Two

"Look up," Diane said. "Look at all those balloons."

Two large nets filled with colorful balloons were tied to the ceiling of the gym.

Ten players, five from each team, stood on the court. The Hamilton players wore orange and black uniforms; the players from the other team, Franklin High School, wore green and yellow uniforms. Two players, one from each team, stood in the middle of the court. A referee in a black and white striped shirt stood between them. He held a basketball.

Trill! Trill!

The referee blew his whistle. He tossed

the basketball up. The two players jumped. The one from Hamilton got to it first and tapped it to a teammate.

"Hurry! Let's find seats," Mr. Shelton said.

Hundreds of people had come to the game. Almost every seat in the bleachers was taken.

Cam looked up. She saw someone in the last row waving. It was Danny. There were empty seats in his row.

Hamilton scored and the crowd cheered.

Cam and the Sheltons climbed to the last row. They were just below the balloons.

Donna told Danny, "We're winning!"

"No we're not," Danny said. "Franklin just scored. We're tied, two to two."

"Oh, I want Hamilton to win," Donna said.

"Me, too," Diane said. "Go Hamilton!" she shouted.

The players ran from one end of the court to the other. They passed the ball. They carefully threw it toward the basket.

"They go so fast," Donna said. "Sometimes I can't tell who has the ball."

"Watch our number twelve," Mr. Shelton said. "That's Jordan Gold. He's the best player on the team."

The score kept changing. First Hamilton was winning. Then Franklin was ahead.

Bzzz!

A buzzer sounded.

Eric's baby brother Howie cried.

"The noise scared him," Mrs. Shelton said. She gave Howie a pacifier.

"Is the game over?" Diane asked. "Did we lose?"

"No," Mrs. Shelton answered. "Franklin is ahead, but it's just the end of the first half."

"It's like recess at school," Danny explained. "It's a good time for some jokes."

Danny pointed to the balloons and asked, "Do you know what the balloon said when it met the pin?"

"I think Howie is hungry," Mr. Shelton said.

Donna took a bottle from the bag and gave it to her father.

"We're behind by three," Mr. Pace told Danny. "But don't worry. When I played on the team we were behind lots of times by more than that and we still won."

"Hey," Danny said. "What about my balloon joke?"

"Look!" Diane shouted. "They're back!"

"Go Hamilton!" people shouted.

Danny said, "I'll tell you what the balloon said when it met the pin. It said 'Hi, Buster.' And do you know what you call a crate full of ducks? It's a box of quackers."

Diane said, "Those jokes aren't funny."

"How about this one?" Danny asked. "Do you know what part of a tree scares cats? It's the bark."

Diane shook her head. She didn't think Danny's jokes were funny.

"Don't you get it?" Danny asked. "Dogs bark and a tree has bark."

"Stop telling me jokes," Diane said. "I'm watching the game."

It was an exciting game. There were lots of short passes between players. There were a few long passes, too, from one end of the court to the other.

Players tried to get close to the basket before they took a shot. But near the end of the game, Jordan Gold took a shot from almost the middle of the court. He got it in. Then he missed a shot from just a few feet away.

"This is it," Mr. Shelton said. "There's less than one minute to go."

Cam looked at the scoreboard. The score was fifty-two to fifty-one. Franklin was winning.

"Franklin has the ball," Danny's father said sadly. "They just have to hold on to it to win the game."

The Franklin player with the ball bounced it a few times. Then he passed it to another Franklin player. The other player bounced the ball a few times and passed it back.

This time the ball never reached his teammate!

Jordan Gold jumped in and grabbed it. He threw the ball all the way down the court to Hamilton's number eight, who was standing near the basket. Number eight took the easy shot and scored.

Bzzz!

The buzzer sounded. The game was over. Hamilton had won!

Fans stood. They cheered.

Two of the Hamilton players lifted Coach Jenkins onto their shoulders. They carried him to one of the baskets. He cut off the net as a souvenir of his last game.

The players carried Coach Jenkins to a microphone set in the middle of the court. They put the coach down. He stood before the microphone ready to speak. The cheering crowd was suddenly quiet.

"Thank you," Coach Jenkins said. "Thanks for thirty happy years."

People cheered.

"Thank you for letting me stay in high school for so long with so many great young people. It's helped me feel young, too."

A Hamilton Helper climbed up the bleachers past Cam and Eric. He was holding a pair of scissors. He was about to cut the net and release the balloons.

"Not yet," Jordan Gold called out.

Jordan Gold stepped up to the microphone. "This is the game ball," he said, and gave the coach a basketball. "We've all signed it."

"Thank you again," Coach Jenkins said.

The crowd cheered.

Jordan Gold held up his hands.

"We have another surprise for you."

"I know what it is," Diane said. "That boy will cut the net and all the balloons will fall out."

"That's not it," Mr. Shelton told her. "I heard the sports news this afternoon. One of Coach's old players is coming here. He has a special gift for Coach."

"Is it you?" Donna asked her father. "Did you bring something?"

"Oh, I bet it's you," Diane said to Mr. Pace. "I bet you're going to show everyone that you're wearing your orange shirt."

"No," Mr. Shelton answered. "It's someone real famous."

"Shh," Mrs. Shelton told him. "Don't tell them. Let the children be surprised."

The side doors of the gym opened. Four guards walked in. They looked around. Then they turned to the open doors and waved.

"Here he comes," Mr. Shelton said. "Here he comes!"

Chapter Three

A tall man walked into the gym. He was followed by a man and a woman. The tall man raised both his hands over his head and waved. People cheered.

"Who is he?" Diane asked.

"That's Governor Zellner," Mr. Shelton said. "He went to Hamilton High School. He was on the basketball team."

"Who are the man and woman who walked in after him?" Donna asked.

"They must be his assistants, his helpers," Mrs. Shelton said.

Governor Zellner and Coach Jenkins hugged. Then the governor stepped up to the microphone.

Players from both teams got close to the governor and the coach. The governor's four guards got close, too.

"It is a joy for me to be here to honor Coach Jenkins," Governor Zellner said. "I played for Coach. He is one of the finest men in our state. I was proud to wear a Hamilton orange and black uniform."

People cheered.

Governor Zellner held up his hands again and they were quiet.

He turned to Coach Jenkins and told him, "I have a special gift for you."

"This will be great," Mr. Shelton said.

One of the governor's assistants went outside. She came back carrying a large box.

"I bet it's a car," Diane said.

"No," Donna told her. "A car wouldn't fit in that box."

"But car keys would," Diane said.

The assistant gave the box to Governor Zellner. The governor opened it and took out a basketball.

"For the past year I have taken this basketball with me as I traveled throughout the state. It was signed by more than one hundred of your former players."

The governor pointed to a spot on the ball. "Look here," he said. "Matt Taylor, the famous actor, signed it."

Coach Jenkins laughed. "He's a great actor, but he wasn't a very good basketball player."

Governor Zellner said, "Toby Coleman, the great artist, signed it. He drew a little picture on it, too."

Coach Jenkins looked at the picture and said, "Wow! It's like his famous line and circle paintings."

Governor Zellner smiled. "I signed it, too. I'm the governor and one day I hope to be president."

Coach Jenkins smiled and said, "And you were a pretty good basketball player."

People cheered.

A few people shouted, "Zellner for president!"

Coach Jenkins and Governor Zellner put the two basketballs on a bench at the edge of the court. Then they hugged.

People left their seats and surrounded the governor and the coach. The Hamilton Helper standing by Cam and Eric cut the two nets. Hundreds of balloons fell out. They fell onto the bleachers and onto the court.

Danny caught one of the balloons. "Just call me Buster," Danny said. Then he stepped on the balloon.

Pop!

"Please," Jordan Gold shouted into the microphone. "Please join us at the party. It's in the cafeteria."

Danny said, "I love parties."

Children and their parents hurried through the door toward the cafeteria. Danny and his father started down the stands.

"Let's go!" Donna said.

"No, let's stay," Diane said. "It's so pretty looking at all the balloons."

Diane looked out across the gym. Then she asked Cam, "Please, take a picture for me."

Cam looked at all the people and the colorful balloons. She blinked her eyes and said, *"Click!"*

"Now let me see it," Diane said. "Let me see the picture."

"You can't," Eric told her. "Only Cam can see the pictures in her head."

"That's not fair," Diane said. Then she turned to her parents and said, "Let's go."

The Hamilton players followed their coach and Governor Zellner out of the gym. The Franklin players went the other way, into the locker room.

The Sheltons followed Danny down toward the gym floor. When Cam and Eric got to the bottom, Eric said, "Look! One of the governor's assistants is looking around. I think something is missing."

Cam closed her eyes. She said, *"Click!"*

Cam looked at the picture she had in her head of the coach and governor. She looked at the pictures she had of the people in the gym, all the seats, and the benches.

Cam opened her eyes. "Look at that bench," she told Eric. "There's just one basketball on it. Was Coach Jenkins carrying one of the basketballs when he left the gym?"

"I don't know," Eric said.

Cam closed her eyes and said, *"Click!"* again.

"He wasn't," Cam said and opened her eyes. "He wasn't carrying a basketball."

"Then one of the signed basketballs is missing," Eric said. "I bet it's the one the governor brought, the one Matt Taylor signed. That's why the governor's assistant is looking around."

Chapter Four

"The basketball signed by the governor, Matt Taylor, and that artist is real valuable," Eric said. "I bet it was stolen."

"Maybe not," Cam told him. "It may have fallen off the bench. With all the balloons on the floor, it's hard to tell. Or maybe one of the guards has it."

One of the governor's guards was standing by the side door. The governor's assistant was looking around. Everyone else had left the gym.

Cam and Eric walked down to the floor of the gym. On their way, they kicked aside lots of balloons. They stopped by the bench at the edge of the court. Eric picked up the basketball. He looked at all the signatures.

"Matt Taylor's name isn't on here. There are no lines and circles," Eric said. "This is the one signed by the team."

"Put that down."

Eric turned. The governor's assistant was walking toward him. She was a tall woman with long red hair.

Eric put the ball on the bench.

Cam told the assistant, "The ball signed by Governor Zellner is missing."

"Please, go to the cafeteria with the other children."

Cam told her, "I don't think Coach Jenkins had the other basketball when he left the gym. Does one of the guards have it?"

"You may be right," the assistant said.

She wore an earpiece. Attached to it was a small speaker. "Max, Fred, Amy, Jane," she said into the speaker. "Does one of you have a basketball?"

She put her hand to the earpiece. She waited for each of them to answer. Then she asked, "The one the governor brought is not here. If you don't have it, where is it?"

She listened again and then said, "Yes, I'll look for it and get back to you." Then she told Cam and Eric, "You should go to the party. I'll take care of this."

Cam said, "It must have rolled off the bench. It's got to be mixed in with all these balloons. My friend and I are good at finding things."

Eric said, "We'll stay out of your way."

The assistant was not listening to Cam and Eric. She was busy kicking aside balloons and looking under the benches at the side of the court.

Cam said to Eric, "It might have rolled under the bleachers. Let's look there."

"I don't think it rolled anywhere," Eric whispered. "I think someone took it."

Beneath the bleachers were long metal poles supporting the seats. Lots of balloons had fallen there. There were papers and candy wrappers, too.

Cam and Eric walked slowly between the metal poles.

"Look," Eric said. He bent to pick up something. "I found a dime."

Cam looked among the balloons. Eric searched through everything on the floor. They came out at the other end of the bleachers.

"Look what I found," Eric said. He showed Cam a handful of coins. "Sixty-four cents. I'll share it with you."

"Thanks. But we didn't find the basketball."

Eric told Cam, "We each get thirty-two cents."

The assistant had left the gym. The guard was still standing by the side door. Cam told him they had looked under the bleachers but did not find the basketball.

"Max, Amy, Jane," the guard said into his speaker. "The ball is not under the bleachers. I don't think it's in here."

He held his hand to the earpiece. He listened for a moment.

"Yes, Max," he said. "I'll watch the gym and the door. No one will leave here with that ball."

The guard turned to Cam and Eric. "Why don't you go to the cafeteria. It's a real party with lots of ice cream and cake. Don't worry. We'll find that basketball."

Cam and Eric walked toward the cafeteria.

"He's wrong," Eric whispered to Cam as they walked. "They won't find that basketball. We will!"

Chapter Five

Two Hamilton Helpers were standing in the hall.

"The party is in the cafeteria," one of them told Cam and Eric. "It's at the end of this hall."

"Did you see anyone walk by with a basketball?" Eric asked. "One is missing."

"People rushed past us," one of the helpers said. "We couldn't see everyone. Ten of them may have had basketballs."

"Maybe twenty," the other helper said. "We're just pointing the way to the party."

Cam asked, "Is there another way out of the gym?"

"No. The gym door to the parking lot is closed. We want everyone to go to the party."

"And there's a guard by the side door," the other student said. "No one can leave there. That's where the governor's car is parked."

"But what about the Franklin players?" Cam asked. "They went through another door."

"They went to the locker room to take showers and get dressed. But they can't leave from there."

"That's right," the other helper said. "Everyone has to walk past us to get to the party. They can leave from the cafeteria."

"Thank you," Cam and Eric both said.

They walked ahead and Eric whispered, "Then whoever took the basketball must have gone through the cafeteria."

Cam and Eric stopped by the entrance to the cafeteria. It was crowded. Most of the people stood by tables. Cake and ice cream and bottles of juice and soda were on the tables. Balloons hung from the ceiling. The walls were decorated with lots of THANKS COACH! signs.

Eric pointed to the far end of the cafeteria and said, "There's someone standing by the door. She's wearing an orange Hamilton Helper sash. She'll know if someone left here with the basketball."

Cam and Eric slowly walked through the crowded room.

"Did you have some cake?" Donna asked Eric.

"Not now," he told his sister. "I'm busy."

Danny's father was standing by a table near the middle of the room. He was wearing the top of his very tight orange uniform. Danny was in front of him.

"Look at me," Danny said to Cam and Eric. He had put buttercream icing from the

cake under his chin and nose. "I'm Old King Cole!"

"That's cute," Cam said as they squeezed past Danny.

Some Hamilton players were talking with Coach Jenkins and Governor Zellner. The players were still in their uniforms.

Eric whispered, "Look how tall they are."

Cam and Eric walked past them.

"I feel like I just walked past a redwood forest," Eric whispered. "And those Hamilton basketball players are the tall redwood trees."

Eric turned and looked back at the players. He laughed and said, "They got all sweaty playing basketball. Those players are trees who need showers."

At last, Cam and Eric were by the exit to the parking lot.

Eric asked the helper, "Did anyone leave here carrying a signed basketball?"

"I wouldn't let anyone leave with that," she said. "And anyway, no one has left. This party is just getting started."

Cam and Eric turned and looked at the crowded cafeteria.

"If no one left," Eric said, "then someone here must have that ball."

Cam said, "A basketball is big and round. It's not easy to hide."

They looked across the room.

People were holding plates with cake and ice cream. Lots of people were talking with Coach Jenkins. There was a line of people waiting to talk with Governor Zellner.

"Hey," Eric said. "Look at her. She might be hiding the basketball under her shirt."

He pointed to a woman with a large round stomach.

Cam laughed. "I think there's a baby in there. I think she's pregnant."

"Oh."

Then Eric pointed to a bag by one of the tables. Then he shook his head and told Cam, "I almost did it again. I was about to tell you that bag is big enough to hold a basketball. But it's our bag! It's got all Howie's baby stuff."

Jordan Gold stood on a chair. He held up his hands and called out, "It's time to let Coach know how much we love him. Let's all sing 'For He's a Jolly Good Fellow.'"

Governor Zellner stood on a chair, too.

The Hamilton team's best player and the governor waved their arms and led everyone as they sang.

Eric told Cam, "My dad said Coach Jenkins really is a good fellow. My dad loved playing for him."

When the song was done, people gathered around the coach. They shook his hand. They hugged him.

Eric said, "I really want to find Coach Jenkins's basketball."

"So do I," Cam said. "If it was stolen, then that's wrong. And anyway, when there's a mystery, I like to solve it."

Eric told Cam, "I'm sure you'll find it."

Cam looked again across the room. She didn't see anyone holding a bag or box large enough for a basketball.

Cam shook her head.

"You may be sure," she told Eric, "but I'm not."

Chapter Six

"Let's walk through the room again," Cam said. "Someone here must be hiding that ball."

Cam and Eric slowly walked away from the door. Cam looked to the right. Eric looked to the left.

"We were losing by twelve points," Cam heard one man tell another. "And do you know who led the team to victory? It was Governor Elliot Zellner."

"I want more cake," Eric heard a child tell his father. "And I want more juice and more ice cream."

Cam and Eric were almost by the entrance

to the cafeteria. They had looked at everyone. No one had a bag or box big enough to hold a basketball. They stopped and turned. They looked across the room.

The Hamilton players were walking toward them. Eric pinched his nose closed.

"They should really take showers," Eric whispered.

"Showers," Cam said. "Of course! Not everyone is at the party. The Franklin players are in the locker room taking showers."

"Good," Eric said. "That's what they should do after a game."

"But they're not here," Cam said. "Maybe one of the Franklin players stole the ball."

The Hamilton players walked past Cam and Eric. They walked into the hall toward the locker room.

Franklin players were leaving the locker room. They had on regular clothes. They were wearing green and yellow school jackets. Each of them carried a small green canvas bag.

"Hey! What's in the bags?" Eric asked.

"Their towels and dirty uniforms are in there," Cam said.

Eric said, "I bet there's something else in one of those bags. I bet the signed basketball is in one of them."

"I don't think so," Cam said. "Those bags are much too small."

Cam and Eric followed the Hamilton players.

The players from the two teams met in the middle of the hall.

"Hi," Jordan Gold said to the Franklin players. "You played a good game."

"Thanks. How is the party?"

"It's great," Jordan Gold answered. "We're just going to clean up. Then we're going back. Wait for us."

Eric poked at one of the canvas bags.

A tall Franklin player looked down at Eric and asked, "What are you doing?"

Eric looked up and said, "I just wondered what basketball players keep in these bags."

The player laughed. "Dirty clothes," he said, and unzipped the bag.

Eric looked in. There was a blue towel in the bag and a green and yellow Franklin uniform.

The players from the two teams talked about the game and Coach Jenkins.

Cam looked at all the gym bags. She was right. They were all much too small to hold a basketball.

"We'll see you at the party," Jordan Gold told the Franklin players.

Eric watched Jordan Gold and the other Hamilton players walk toward the locker room. Cam turned and watched the Franklin players walk toward the cafeteria.

"Hey," Cam whispered. "Look at him." She pointed to a short boy in a green and yellow Franklin jacket. "I don't remember him on the court."

The boy was carrying a small green canvas bag.

Cam closed her eyes. She said, *"Click!"* She said, *"Click!"* again. Then Cam opened her eyes. "I was right," she said. "He's not on the team."

"Then he doesn't have a dirty uniform," Eric said. "Why would he have a canvas bag? I bet he didn't even take a shower."

Cam and Eric followed the Franklin players into the cafeteria.

"But he can't have the ball," Eric whispered. "He's too thin to be hiding it under his shirt. And that bag is too small."

"I know," Cam whispered. "This whole thing is strange. He walked down the hall

with the Franklin players, but they never spoke to him. I don't think they even looked at him. He's pretending to be with the team, but he's not."

Eric asked, "Are you sure he's not on the team?"

Cam nodded her head. She was sure.

"I looked at the pictures I have in my head

of every player on the court," she said. "He's not in even one picture."

The Franklin players took plates of cake and ice cream and cups of juice or soda. But the short boy in the green and yellow jacket didn't. He walked straight through the cafeteria.

"Look at that," Eric whispered. "He's walking right to the exit. That's real strange. I've never seen a teenager walk past free cake and ice cream."

"He's leaving," Cam said, "and we've got to stop him. I'm sure he knows something about the missing basketball."

Chapter Seven

Cam and Eric hurried into the cafeteria. Cam quickly stopped by one of the tables. She took a plate, a large piece of cake, some melted ice cream, and a napkin.

"Get some juice," she told Eric.

"But I'm not thirsty."

"Just get some juice," she told him again. Eric filled a cup with apple juice.

The boy was almost by the exit. Cam caught up to him. She bumped into him and got buttercream icing and melted ice cream on his jacket.

"I'm so sorry," Cam said. "I'll wipe it off."

With the napkin, Cam spread the icing and

the ice cream across the back of his jacket.

The boy twisted his head and looked at the back of his jacket. He turned and told Cam, "You made it worse."

BRIAN was stitched onto the front of his jacket.

"Don't worry, Brian," Cam said. "I'll wash it off."

Cam took the cup of juice from Eric and spilled it on the jacket.

"Hey!" Brian screamed. "Now I smell like apples."

The Sheltons hurried over.

"What happened?" Mrs. Shelton asked. "Why are you shouting? Did my son do something?"

"No," Brian said. "It's your daughter. She got cake stuff and ice cream all over my jacket."

"Oh, she's not my daughter. She's a friend."

"What's the problem?" the Hamilton Helper standing by the door asked.

"This girl got cake and ice cream all over my jacket," Brian shouted.

Mr. Shelton took out his wallet.

Coach Jenkins, Governor Zellner, three of his guards, and his two assistants came over.

"What's wrong?" the tall red-haired assistant asked.

Brian looked at Coach Jenkins, Governor Zellner, his assistants, and the guards.

"I've got to go," Brian said.

"No, wait," Mr. Shelton said. "I'll pay the cleaning bill."

Brian didn't wait. He rushed to the door. He seemed scared. He kicked balloons aside and ran out of the cafeteria.

"Stop him," Cam told the governor's guards. "He knows something about the missing basketball."

Coach Jenkins asked, "What missing basketball?"

"Don't worry," one of the guards told the coach. "We'll find it."

"Find what?" Governor Zellner asked.

"The basketball you signed is missing," the guard said. "It must have rolled off. We'll find it."

"No, you won't," Cam said. "If that boy gets away you won't ever find that basketball."

Cam, Eric, and others hurried to the door. They watched Brian hurry through the parking lot.

"Stop him!" Eric said. "We have to stop him before he gets away."

"Did he take the basketball?" one of the guards asked.

"We think he did," Cam answered.

Governor Zellner said, "We can't stop someone because you think he did something wrong."

Danny pushed into the crowd. He had two balloons and a sharp toothpick.

"Hey, Mr. Governor, do you know who I am?" Danny asked. "I'm 'Buster' Danny." He pointed the toothpick at the balloon and said, "Watch this."

"Not now," Eric told him.

"Yes now," Danny said, and pushed the toothpick into one of the balloons. "This is funny."

Pop!

The busted balloon fell to the floor.

"That's why they call me 'Buster,'" Danny said and pushed the toothpick into the second balloon.

Pop!

The second busted balloon fell to the floor.

Cam looked at the two busted balloons.

"That's it!" Cam said. "I know where the basketball is hidden. And that boy has it!"

"Are you sure?" Governor Zellner asked.

"Yes," Cam told him. "I think I am. I think I know where to find that basketball."

The guards looked at the governor.

"Go ahead," Governor Zellner told the guards. "Tell that boy I want to see him."

Chapter Eight

Two of the guards rushed outside.

"I hope you're right," Governor Zellner told Cam. "I don't want to bring him back here if he did nothing wrong."

"I also hope I'm right," Cam said.

Cam, Eric, and the others watched the two guards run through the parking lot. Brian started running, too, but the guards were too fast for him.

The guards caught up to Brian and talked to him. One stood on one side of Brian. The other guard stood on the other side. They were much taller than Brian.

"Look," Eric said, and pointed. "He's coming back."

Brian walked slowly into the cafeteria. The guards were right behind him. His head was down. He kicked aside some balloons and stood in front of Governor Zellner.

"They said you wanted to talk to me."

"Yes, I do," Governor Zellner said.

Eric said, "Ask him what's in the bag."

"Stuff," he answered. "I didn't do anything wrong. It's not against the law to have stuff, is it?"

"If there's just stuff in your bag," one of the guards said, "you won't mind if we look in it."

Cam said, "I think the 'stuff' you have in that bag is a stolen basketball."

Brian laughed. "A basketball wouldn't fit."

"He's right," Governor Zellner said. "That bag is too small to hold a basketball."

Cam took a balloon off the floor. Cam asked Brian and Governor Zellner, "Do you think I could fit this balloon in my pocket?"

"Of course not," the governor answered. "It's too big."

"Please," she said to Danny, "give me a toothpick."

Danny gave Cam a toothpick. She poked it into the balloon.

Pop!

The balloon broke.

Cam put the broken balloon in her pocket.

"You see," she said. "Without the air, it fits in my pocket. And without the air in the basketball, it would fit in that bag."

"Is that what you did?" Governor Zellner asked Brian.

He didn't answer.

"May I have that?" the governor said.

Brian gave him the bag. Governor Zellner took out a small wrinkled basketball. There were signatures on the ball and a line and circle drawing.

"Yeah! Cam did it again!" Eric said. "She solved another mystery."

Mr. Shelton said, "I bet Brian heard on the news that you were giving Coach a basketball signed by Matt Taylor."

Governor Zellner looked at the many

people who had gathered around him, Coach Jenkins, Cam, Eric, and Brian. Jordan Gold and the other Hamilton players were there, too. They had showered. Now they were dressed in regular clothes.

"I'm calling the police," the governor said. "They'll handle this."

One of the guards took out a cell phone. He called the police.

Governor Zellner gave Coach Jenkins the wrinkled basketball.

The coach laughed. "It's like me," he said. "I've got wrinkles, too."

Cam thought, *It's also like Mr. Shelton. His face has lots of wrinkles.*

"That's easy to fix," Jordan Gold said. "I'll pump it up."

Coach Jenkins gave Jordan Gold the wrinkled basketball.

Governor Zellner turned to Cam and Eric. "People who do good deeds should be rewarded. Now how should I reward you for finding Coach's basketball?"

Coach Jenkins whispered something to the governor.

"That's a good idea," Governor Zellner said.

Coach Jenkins then whispered to Jordan Gold. He gave him some keys.

"Don't forget me," Danny said. "I also helped find the basketball. My buster joke helped Cam solve the mystery."

"Yes," Coach Jenkins said. "Bring three."

Two police cars drove up to school.

Four police officers got out of the cars. They walked into the cafeteria. Governor Zellner told them what Brian had done.

"Come with us," one of the police officers said.

Brian left the cafeteria with the officers. He got into the back of one of the police cars. The two cars drove off.

Jordan Gold came back with the basketball and three orange Hamilton High School sweatshirts. The basketball was filled with air. It didn't have wrinkles.

Jordan Gold gave the governor the three sweatshirts. A guard gave the governor a black marker. Governor Zellner signed each of the shirts.

The guard gave a shirt to Cam, Eric, and Danny.

Danny put on his shirt. He puffed out his stomach and said, "Hey, look. I'm an orange pumpkin."

No one laughed.

"Oh well," Danny said. "My jokes helped Cam solve the mystery. It pays to tell good jokes."

Diane shook her head and said, "You mean it pays to tell bad jokes. It pays to tell real bad jokes."

Cam and Eric laughed. Governor Zellner, Coach Jenkins, and lots of other people looked at Danny with his puffed-out stomach and laughed. Then Danny, the orange pumpkin, laughed, too.

A Cam Jansen Memory Game

Take another look at the picture opposite page 1. Study it. Blink your eyes and say, *"Click!"* Then turn back here and answer the questions at the bottom of the page. Please, first study the picture, *then* look at the questions.

1. Is Mr. Shelton wearing a hat? Eyeglasses?

2. How many people are in the Sheltons' SUV?

3. Who is sitting directly behind Mr. Shelton?

4. What is the baby holding?

5. Are Eric's twin sisters wearing shirts with stripes?

6. Who is holding Mr. Shelton's yearbook, Cam or Eric?